Patricia Coombs

DORRIE AND THE HAUNTED SCHOOLHOUSE

CLARION BOOKS · NEW YORK

Clarion Books
a Houghton Mifflin Company imprint
215 Park Avenue South, New York, NY 10003
Copyright © 1992 by Patricia Coombs

For information about permission to reproduce selections
from this book, write to Permissions,
Houghton Mifflin Company,
215 Park Avenue South, New York, NY 10003.

www.houghtonmifflinbooks.com

Printed in the U.S.A.

Library of Congress Cataloging-in-Publication Data
Coombs, Patricia.
Dorrie and the haunted schoolhouse / by Patricia Coombs
p.   cm.
Summary: Dorrie the little witch goes to school
where she and Dither, a fellow student, cause chaos
when they mix up some spells.
ISBN 0-395-60116-9   PA ISBN 0-618-13053-5
[1. Witches—Fiction. 2. Schools—Fiction.]   I. Title.
PZ7.C7813D1   1992   91-16483
[E]—dc20
CIP
AC

WOZ   10   9   8   7   6   5

This is Dorrie. She is a witch. A little witch. Her hat is always on crooked and her socks never match. She lives with her mother, the Big Witch, and Cook, and her black cat, Gink.

One Monday morning the Big Witch rushed into the kitchen. "Finish your breakfast! Get dressed! You will be late for school!"

"I want *you* to teach me potions and spells," said Dorrie.

"I tried," said the Big Witch. "It gave me a headache. A teacher is someone who doesn't get headaches. Someone like Professor Zucchini. You're going to school."

3

Dorrie went upstairs to her room and Gink went with her. She put on a dress. She put on her best hat. She reached under the bed for her lucky sock. It wasn't there. She pulled everything out of her closet. It wasn't there. She looked under her pillow, and in the wastebasket. She emptied her dresser drawers.

The Big Witch threw open the door. "Hurry! You're making me late!" she cried. "I have to fix the lightning for the Weather Witch in Gloomsbury!"

"I can't find my lucky sock," said Dorrie. "I can't start anything new without my lucky sock. It's a rule."

"GO! NOW!" snapped the Big Witch. "That is *my* rule."

Down, down, down the stairs, out the door, across the yard, and into the woods went Dorrie, with Gink beside her.

"Gink," said Dorrie, "my luck is even worse than I thought. There's a hole in my pocket and my lucky penny fell out. And I forgot our lunch. I wish we were in Gloomsbury helping Mother."

The path zigzagged deeper and deeper into the woods. The shadows grew thicker and thicker. Just when they thought they were lost, Dorrie and Gink saw the old schoolhouse ahead of them among the trees.

Dorrie went inside. A thin witch with glasses and a short, round wizard were standing there. "Dither! Mince!" said Dorrie.

"Aunt Trillium made us come," said Dither.

"Home," said Mince.

"No," said Dither. "We just got here."

Thick gray dust and cobwebs covered old desks and chairs, books and boxes of papers. It was very, very spooky. And very, very still.

All at once a weird howl echoed through the school.

Dorrie and Dither looked at each other. "It's the ghost! The ghost that flunked!" whispered Dither. "He can't get into the next grade, but he hangs around and causes trouble. Aunt Trillium said so."

A pale shape whistled past their ears.

"We'd better find Professor Zucchini," said Dorrie, "quick. He must be upstairs."

9

Up, up, up the creaking stairs they went, and down the hall. The first door was nailed shut. The second door was nailed shut. But the third door was partly open. Inside was a blackboard covered with writing. There was a table with a big cauldron. Jars and bottles and bags of magic were everywhere. A broomstick was propped against a chair. A black, pointed hat with a Z on it hung on the back. But Professor Zucchini was nowhere to be seen.

"Why isn't he here?" said Dither. "Where did he go?"

"I don't know," said Dorrie. "The cauldron is hot, so he must have just left. He was writing on the blackboard. See? The numbers stop and there's a squiggle."

They sat down to wait for Professor Zucchini. They waited and they waited. They got up a dozen times to look out the window to see if he was coming. All they could see was shadows and trees.

The blackboard creaked and groaned. They both stared at it. "Look," said Dorrie. "This part must be for us. It says, Lesson One: Quick Start Broomstick Mix."

"Well," said Dither, "it doesn't look any harder than the recipe for cornmeal muffins I made last night. Let's work on it and surprise the professor."

"That's a very good idea," said Dorrie. "I will read it to you and stir. You can measure out the magic stuff and put it in the cauldron."

"Home," said Mince.

"No," said Dither. "We haven't learned anything yet."

"Okay," said Dorrie. "One-third cup of black powder, a pint of yellow crystals, a tablespoon of toad spit, one firecracker, three cups of eel slime, a pinch…"

"Slow down!" cried Dither. "What comes after the quart of black powder, the three cups of crystals, and the pint of firecrackers?"

"Dither! That's wrong! It's *one-third* cup of black powder and *one* firecracker! Quick! We have to add a lot of the other stuff now." Dorrie reached for the jar of eel slime.

"Oh, no you *don't*," screeched Dither, giving Dorrie a push. "I'M supposed to do this part. You stopped stirring, and look, it's boiling over!"

"You're the one who did it wrong!" cried Dorrie, stirring harder and faster. "You don't even know how to measure!"

"How can I measure when you're splashing that guck all over my glasses?" snapped Dither, dumping in a bag of feathers.

The cauldron was glowing hotter and hotter. All at once there was a *boom* and a flash of light. The potion flowed over the sides of the cauldron. It flooded the table and spilled, bubbling and hissing and steaming, over the floor, into the hall, and down the stairs.

"Make it stop! Make it stop!" shouted Dither.

"ABRACADABRA!" cried Dorrie, banging on the cauldron with the ladle.

It didn't work. The potion kept on flowing. There was a distant cracking sound. The schoolhouse lurched. Another crack, and a loud *whoosh*, and it lifted itself high in the air. Over the woods it sailed. Tilting and spinning, it sped over Witches' Meadow, over Black Pond and the pumpkin fields beyond.

Dorrie and Dither hung on to the windowsill and looked down.

"I think we're in trouble," said Dorrie. "Big trouble."

"Ohhh," wailed Dither. "We're almost over Witchville! Everybody is going to see what we've done!"

In the streets of Witchville, witches and wizards watched the schoolhouse whizzing over the town. It began doing loop-the-loops and figure eights.

"Oo la!" said an old witch. "Our schoolhouse is even more haunted than it used to be."

"A first for Witchville! We're making history!" shouted the News Witch, getting out her notebook.

Dorrie and Dither leaned out the window, yelling for help. But the witches and wizards couldn't hear them.

They waved their arms. The witches and wizards waved back.

The schoolhouse did a tailspin around the Town Tower. The witches and wizards clapped. They cheered. They sent up balloons.

"It's no use," sighed Dorrie. "They think Professor Zucchini is putting on an air show."

Soon Witchville was far behind them. Dorrie and Dither slumped together on the floor. The blackboard creaked and groaned.

"Professor Zucchini is going to be very upset when he finds out what we did to the schoolhouse," said Dorrie. "And Mother is going to be really mad at me."

Dither moaned. "So is Aunt Trillium. She may never let me come to school again. I'll never learn anything harder than muffins."

Dorrie nodded. "I knew I shouldn't start school without my lucky sock."

"Some of this mess is my bad luck, too," said Dither. "Aunt Trillium washed my lucky ribbons yesterday. She washed all the luck out of them."

Dorrie looked around. "We're stuck up here in the air. The Professor is gone. We can't go home. We can't get anybody to help. There is only one thing to do." She opened a book of magic.

"A good luck potion!" cried Dither, opening another book.

They looked and looked. Some of the recipes were too hard. Some of them took weeks to make.

"I found a good one!" said Dorrie. "It looks easy and quick."

They set to work. They wiped out the cauldron and cleaned the ladle. They cleared the table.

"This time we won't make any mistakes," said Dorrie. "We won't argue. I will read slowly and give you lots of time."

"I will measure the magic carefully," said Dither. "If I don't understand something, we'll figure it out together."

23

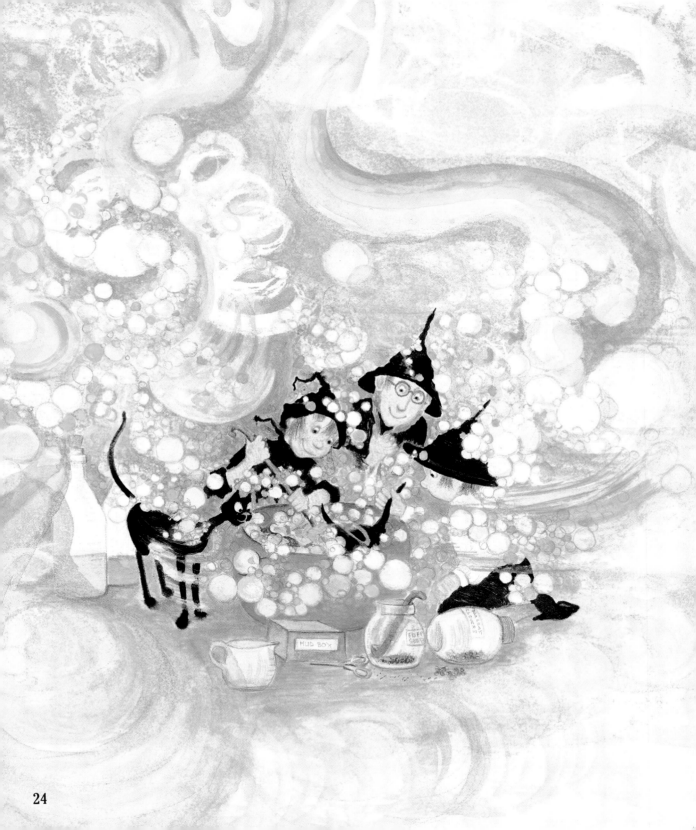

They spoke in whispers as they worked. Soon they had everything ready: a cup of salt, a pint of four-leaf clovers, a quart of dew, a silver spoon, a nutmeg, and a lump of coal. They had a splinter from a ladder, mud from a wizard's shoe, and a handful of poppyseeds.

"Now it's time for the handful of witches' hair," whispered Dorrie. She snipped off part of her bangs. Dither cut the end off one of her braids. They sprinkled the hair over the potion.

Together they began to stir. The cauldron glowed pink, then red, then orange. The handle of the ladle hummed under their fingers. The steam floated in rainbows all around them. They counted to ten.

"Now!" said Dorrie. She pulled off a sock and dropped it into the cauldron. Dither put her ribbons in. Mince tossed in his vest. Dorrie rubbed some of the potion on Gink's paws. Last of all, they dropped in the professor's black pointed hat.

By turns, they counted to nine hundred and nine until the cauldron had cooled to black again. Then Dorrie pulled out her new lucky sock and put it on. It was still warm, and it smelled like clover and nutmeg. Dither tied on her ribbons, and Mince put on his vest. Dorrie took the professor's black hat and hung it on the blackboard frame.

"It's working! I can feel the luckiness all over me!" said Dither.

"Me, too!" said Dorrie. "But it is awfully late. The sun is starting to set. Nobody will be able to see us..."

Suddenly the blackboard let out a long groan. It was shivering and quivering. It began to sag. Slowly it slid off the wall into a pile of lumpy blackness. As they watched, a hand came out of it, then an arm, then another arm, and then the rest of the body stood up.

"Professor Zucchini!" they cried.

"My dear students!" he shouted. "You saved me in the nick of time with this wonderful good luck hat!"

"Now could you please save all of us," said Dorrie. "From Lesson One. We don't know how to get down."

"Yes! Yes! We need more gravity around here," said the professor. "Stay in line behind me and do exactly what I do. One, two, three, go!"

Up and down the halls they went, chanting and making signs in the air. Slowly the rooms filled up with lavender light. The schoolhouse began spinning down, down, down out of the sky. It landed with a thump in the middle of Witches' Meadow.

"Look where we are!" cried Dither, running to the door.

"Very nice!" said the professor. "Much better light than in the woods."

"And much closer to my house," said Dorrie. "Let's go have tea."

The Big Witch was glad to see them. Professor Zucchini told them all how he'd turned himself into a blackboard. "Just as I was writing down a formula for brain waves, the ghost howled in my ear. Instead of *three*, I wrote *Z*. If Dorrie and Dither hadn't changed my luck before sunset, I'd have been a blackboard forever. They did good work!"

"I like school a lot," said Dorrie. "Especially now that it's in Witches' Meadow."

"School! Good luck! Ghost! Blackboard!" said Mince.

"Mince learned five words today!" said Dither. "He never wanted to say anything except 'home' until now. Aunt Trillium will be so pleased."

Cook came in with a tray of sandwiches and cookies. An orange sock was hanging out of her pocket.

"You found my old lucky sock!" cried Dorrie. "Where was it?"

The Big Witch looked at her. "It was tied to my old broomstick, which was in the lilac bush."

"I was practicing," said Dorrie. "If you taught me to fly, I could fly to school."

"Well, that might be a better idea," said the Big Witch, "than flying the school."